SO-CWV-497

EARTH INSPECTORS™

— ③ —

OLYMPUS!

What is the secret of the Oracle?

by Edward Packard

Illustrations by Barbara Carter

McGRAW-HILL BOOK COMPANY

New York St. Louis San Francisco Auckland Bogotá Hamburg
London Madrid Mexico Milan Montreal New Delhi
Panama Paris São Paulo Singapore Sydney Tokyo Toronto

EARTH INSPECTORS is a trademark of Metabooks, Inc.
Original conception by Edward Packard.

1 2 3 4 5 6 7 8 9 SEM SEM 8 9 2 1 0 9 8

ISBN 0-07-047995-X

LIBRARY OF CONGRESS CATALOGING-IN-PUBLICATION DATA

Packard, Edward, 1931–
    Olympus: what is the secret of the Oracle? by Edward Packard.
        p. cm.
    Summary: As an Earth Inspector, the reader travels back in time to
Greece in 400 B.C. to search out the Oracle of Delphi and discover the
secret of her powers.
    ISBN 0-07-047995-X
    1. Plot-your-own stories.   [1. Plot-your-own stories.
2. Oracles—Fiction. 3. Space and time—Fiction. 4. Greece—
Fiction.]   I. Title
PZ7.P124501   1988
[Fic]—dc19

OLYMPUS

Dear Reader,

Are there really aliens in outer space? Most scientists think it likely. And many people have tried to guess what they would be like.

If they were very intelligent and had invented spaceships, they might want to see what's happening here. After all, Earth is a *very* interesting planet.

Imagine how an alien would feel, after traveling trillions of miles in a spacecraft, to see a beautiful blue-white sphere growing larger and larger in the star-studded black sky.

Imagine *you* are that alien—one far more advanced than any human. Your home is on Turoc, fifth planet of the star Bellatrix, which from Earth can be seen in the constellation of Orion.

From time to time as you're reading this book you'll have to make decisions. Whenever you do, turn to the page shown and keep reading. Just remember: Earth is a dangerous planet. So, think before you act, and good luck to you. You are one of the luckiest of Turonians: You are an Earth Inspector!

Edward Packard

EARTH INFORMATION
DATA BANK 3.14159265

Earth Place: Greece
Earth Time: 400 B.C.

Special words:

Acropolis – the prominent hill in a city; notably that in Athens

Agora – the marketplace in a town or city

chiton – a loose cloth garment

frieze – a sculptured, decorated band on a building

hubris – arrogance; foolish pride

Olympus – the highest mountain of Greece— home of the Greek gods; home of any exceptional people

Olympians – the Greek gods, or any exceptional people

Oracle – this is one of those words that means two different things: An Oracle is a priestess or other person who can reveal hidden truths, including truths about the future; an Oracle is also the shrine or other place where such truths are revealed.

Pantheon – a temple dedicated to all the gods

Parthenon – the temple of the goddess Athena atop the Acropolis in Athens

pediment – the triangular gable of a low-pitched roof

Mt. Olympus

Delphi
Itea
Thebes
GULF OF CORINTH
Eleusis
Corinth
Athens
Epidaurus
Piraeus

Peloponnesus

Olympia

NORTH

Sparta

SCALE OF MILES
0   25   50   75   100

A graceful figure leaps through the portal to the Chamber of Wisdom. It is Simbar, the Surveyor of the Spheres. He greets you with a pure harmonic chord. "I am glad you can undertake this mission."

As Simbar speaks, his great eyes shrink to the size of Earth people's eyes, and the fur on his head changes into dark hair. His legs grow longer and his mouth broadens. An odd sound escapes his mouth—a laugh!

"Do not be alarmed by my appearance," he says. "This is the way Earth people look. And the way you too will look, when you are among them."

"With all respect, sir, you have—they have—strange bodies. It's a wonder they don't fall over."

Simbar takes an awkward step toward you. "A good observation, my young friend. It is quite true: Earth has much stronger gravity than Turoc. Standing on two legs there is not easy. Earth people took millions of years to learn this trick. Most creatures on that planet have four legs, and the most numerous clan—the insects—have six."

"I guess I can learn to stand and walk instead of glide and leap," you say.

Approaching Greece from Space

"Do not worry the slightest bit," Simbar says in a kindly tone. "You are bioformed to stand with ease, and walk, and run, and assume this strange human form you see me in, and speak any language on Earth, and appear at any time you wish in that planet's history. Such is the power of Turoc!"

"I have seen our data about Earth," you say. "It is surely one of the most interesting planets in the galaxy."

"Indeed it is," Simbar replies. "And that is why only the boldest and wisest of the Turonians can be Earth Inspectors."

"What is my mission, Simbar?"

"You are to land in Greece—a small country in southeastern Europe."

"Should I just look around and report back?"

"Definitely not. We have already gathered much information—as you have learned. But there are many mysteries we have not solved. For example, there's something happening on Earth that seems to defy the laws of science!" Simbar pauses a moment to scratch his new Earthling chin. "Excuse me. These whiskers are itchy. Anyway, here is the problem. We've received a report of a woman in Greece—a famous Oracle—who foretells the future. Given the primitive state of things on Earth, we don't see how that is possible."

"Are you sure she's not a quack? I've heard there are lots of people on Earth who claim to have special powers. Earthlings tend to be gullible, after all.''

''That is true,'' Simbar says. ''But a lot of smart Greeks believe that *this* Oracle speaks the truth. Reports are that she's never been proven wrong.''

''It sounds like something we should investigate,'' you say.

''Exactly.'' Simbar presses a button and projects a hologram of Earth before your eyes. ''I want you to find out how this woman predicts the future. Just what is her secret?''

Simbar rests his hands on your shoulders—shoulders that have suddenly grown broader. Your arms and legs, too, have been growing into those of an Earth person. ''Good luck, my friend.'' His voice sounds as if he were in a great hollow chamber. ''Remember the wisdom of Turoc, and you shall have the power of Turoc!''

Suddenly he is gone.

Walking like the Earthling you have become, you leave the Chamber of Wisdom and proceed to your spacecraft, which is named after one of Earth's first spacecraft—the *Voyager*. You slide the hatch shut, then check your pack to make sure you have a few extra clothes, your map and compass, and a supply of ancient Greek coins.

Chin Chin, your computron, has his ready light on.

''*Transit*,'' you say softly.

*   *   *

As you move through time and space, your trip lasts only moments in your mind before one yellow-white star grows far brighter than the rest. It is Earth's star—which Earthlings call the "sun." Then Earth itself, wrapped in a net of swirling white clouds, appears in your view port. It grows rapidly larger as the *Voyager* approaches with lightning speed.

Soon the Earth's surface fills half the sky. Below you lies all of Greece, a rugged, mostly forested land bathed in bright sunlight. On three sides it is cradled by blue waters. Snow lies on the mountains to the north. To the east, hundreds of islands seem to float upon the sea. The *Voyager* cruises over a fertile plain in Peloponnesus.

"That's Olympia down there, where the ancient Olympic games were held," says Chin Chin. "It's as good a place to land as any."

"Set us down," you order.

You brace yourself as the *Voyager* gracefully settles in a field near the ruins of a colossal temple. You step out and gaze at the great stone columns lying scattered among the weeds. The sun is just dipping below the trees. You sniff the air, fragrant with flowers. Suddenly you remember you could be noticed at any moment, and quickly transform your spacecraft into a boulder.

You've hardly taken your first step when a big

black dog charges you, barking ferociously. You scramble up on the same boulder that was so recently the *Voyager*. The dog stands growling below, not quite willing to risk a kick in the snout. An elderly man is hurrying toward you.

"Peponi!" he yells.

The dog growls one last time and runs off.

"Hello, my friend," the man calls to you as you jump down. "Peponi had no business chasing you! I, Theodoros Petaras, will make up for his rudeness. Come join my wife and me for refreshment."

You gladly accept the invitation, and Theodoros leads you to a small stone cottage. Bright green vines with pink and blue flowers cling to its whitewashed plaster walls.

Theodoros no sooner introduces you to his wife, Melina, than she places a wooden tray before you. On it are soft walnuts, tiny tomatoes, and pastries stuffed with fruit. It looks like nothing ever served on Turoc, but it's delicious just the same.

Theodoros gives you a glass of cool spring water. He clinks his glass to yours, and you clink back.

"*Yia sas*—to your health," he says.

"*Yia sas!*" you reply.

Your hosts serve you a dinner of lamb and rice, honey cakes and pears, and then, as if they had not already been kind enough, invite you to stay overnight. Before going to bed you ask them about the secret of the Oracle.

"To learn *that* you would have to travel back to when the Oracle was at the height of its powers," says Theodoros.

Melina nods. "Yes—about four hundred B.C., I should say."

"It's a shame such a thing is not possible," says Theodoros with a laugh.

You laugh too, but in the morning, after thanking your hosts and wishing them good fortune, you return to the field where you landed, barely outrunning Peponi in time to retransform your spacecraft and dive inside.

"We must reenter space time, Chin Chin," you say. *"Transit."*

Passing through the space-time continuum, you are hardly conscious of change, until you notice that the landscape below is much more heavily forested than it was before. Beneath you is Greece as it was more than 2300 years before Theodoros and Melina were born!

Suddenly an idea comes to mind.

"What about the Greek gods, Chin Chin? Is it possible they have something to do with the secret of the Oracle?"

"I suppose it's possible," your computron

replies. "People here think that immortal gods live on top of Mount Olympus, and since it's too steep for anyone to climb, no one really can say that they aren't up there."

"Let's fly over Mount Olympus, Chin Chin. I'd like to see it."

Your computron doesn't reply, but a change in the motion of your spacecraft tells you that it is following out your request. In a few moments the famous peak lies before you, or as much as you can see, for the summit is covered with clouds. What a letdown! You've almost decided to quit when the clouds suddenly part. Then you gasp at the sight before you—an enormous palace, which miraculously opens up, revealing the whole pantheon of gods!

In the center, at the top of seven steps, each enameled in a color of the rainbow, sits mighty Zeus on a throne of black marble inlaid with gold. Perched on his arm is a golden eagle with ruby eyes, clutching in its talons shiny, jagged strips of tin, the mighty weapon Zeus uses to hurl thunderbolts at whomever he chooses. Next to the king of the gods is his queen—Hera. Her ivory throne, set at the top of three crystal stairs, is decorated with golden cuckoos and willow leaves. Zeus and Hera are shouting at each other, and even Hera's cuckoos are wailing and screeching at the king of the gods. From what you've learned on Turoc, they are probably fighting over the way Zeus has been misbehaving himself!

"These gods certainly aren't perfect, Chin Chin," you say.

"They are more like big brothers and sisters than ideal fathers and mothers," he replies.

Casting your eyes about at the other gods seated on their thrones, you recognize Poseidon, the god of the sea, Athena, the goddess of wisdom, and Aphrodite, the goddess of love and beauty. Opposite her sits Ares, the cruel god of war. You wonder how Apollo, god of music and poetry, can bear to sit next to him!

Suddenly the clouds close in, and the vision is gone.

"Chin Chin, I can't believe those gods really exist."

"Actually they don't," he says. "That was a holographic projection of mine, assembled from our data bank."

"I thought so! Don't do something like that again without telling me first!"

"All right," Chin Chin says. "But remember—Simbar himself programmed me to be mischievous to keep you on your toes!"

"Well, that's enough mischief for this trip," you say. "Let's land now—and not on top of that mountain!"

The *Voyager* descends so fast you hardly have

time to see the city of Athens and its many splendid buildings. Your craft swiftly sets down, jolting you as it tilts on uneven, rocky ground.

Stepping outside, you take in a breath of cool fresh air—Earth air—and stand awhile looking at the trees and rocks and hills and the brilliant blue sky. Then you call upon the power of Turoc and transform the *Voyager* into a slate-gray boulder.

At the crest of a ridge above you is a dirt road, which your compass tells you must lead to Athens. You shiver a moment, for you are now alone, without your spacecraft or even a computer, on a strange planet in a strange body with only a few extra clothes and supplies and a little Greek money to get by on.

You start up the slope, wobbling a bit as you learn to use your Earth legs. When you reach the road, you set out toward the city, eager to meet the Greeks and to learn the secret of the Oracle.

As you walk along the rough dirt road, you gaze at the hill that rises steeply on your left. Only a few scraggly pines cling to crevices in its rocky face. Looking into the valley on your right, you see goats grazing, and beyond them an Earth dwelling—an adobe house set near a trickling stream. Chickens are pecking at seeds scattered in front of the door.

You climb the hill and round a bend in the

road, and suddenly all of Athens lies before you: a city of houses, shops, and larger buildings— some of them two or three stories high—faced with fluted columns and painted a dozen differ- ent shades. Within this city is a high, flat-topped hill. On top of it—silhouetted against the sky—is an enormous building made of white marble and supported by a row of pillars on each side. Its pediment is adorned with paintings and statues. From your studies on Turoc, you know that the hill must be the Acropolis and the great building atop it is the Parthenon—the Temple of Athena.

You are wearing sandals and a chiton, so you look like any Greek on his way to market or to his workshop, and you can speak Greek as well as anyone, thanks to the power of Turoc. On the other hand, you have no idea how to find the Oracle.

Two donkeys, pulling a cart, are coming up the road. A farmer follows on foot.

"Friend," you call to him, "can you tell me how I can find the Oracle?"

"Which Oracle?" the farmer replies. "For there are many—even here in Athens."

"The most important one," you say.

"Then you must mean the Oracle of Delphi— the sacred Oracle of Apollo. Well, you'll have a long journey to get there. And the priests may not let you see the Oracle when you arrive.

Naturally, almost everyone would like to question the Oracle, but she only speaks to a few people each day."

One of the donkeys starts forward, and its master runs back to his cart and yells at it to stop. A much bigger wagon, loaded with logs and drawn by four oxen, is approaching.

"I must be on my way," the farmer calls to you over his shoulder.

"But can you tell me how to find the Oracle of Delphi?"

"Go to the Parthenon—on the Acropolis. The priests there would know. Or ask someone in the marketplace—the *Agora*."

The farmer is suddenly on his way. You hear a sound and whirl around. The team of oxen has stopped behind you. An elderly man with a sun-beaten, leathery face looks down from his perch on the cart.

"Did I hear you want to get to Delphi?"

"Yes, sir," you answer.

"You'll arrive faster if you travel by boat for most of your journey. After you visit Athens, go to the port of Piraeus. You'll find your way to Delphi, all right, but you better know what to say when you get there!" He smacks his oxen with a stick, and they lumber on, leaving you standing alone by the side of the road.

You continue on to Athens. As you approach

the city gates, an old woman in a black shawl holds out her hand to you. You give her a coin.

"What do you seek in Athens?" she asks.

"Knowledge," you say, "so that I can talk to the Oracle at Delphi and learn her secret."

The woman's face crinkles as she smiles. "You are seeking a great deal. Very few people learn the secret of the Oracle. You *will* need certain knowledge, it's true. For that you might wish to talk to Socrates, the famous philosopher, and Thucydides, the historian. Or see a play by Sophocles. Any of these may do."

The woman turns away, and you continue on. There is something about her that convinces you she is telling you the truth. But how can you meet these men or see such a play? Perhaps it's best to go first to the Parthenon or the Agora, as the farmer you met on the road suggested.

If you go to the Parthenon, go on to the next page.

If you go to the Agora, turn to page 17.

To reach the Parthenon you must climb to the top of the Acropolis. Thinking of this makes you wonder why you couldn't have been transformed into an eagle instead of a human. Then you could have *flown* to the Acropolis. But eagles can't talk, you remember.

A man on horseback approaches. A dozen or so other men are walking behind him, each of them carrying a heavy load of wood. From what you have learned on Turoc, you know these people must be slaves. The horseman looks at you suspiciously. You hurry on as if you were on an important errand. Having no connections to an established family, you could be carried away into slavery at any time.

Turn to page 21.

You have no trouble finding the Agora—the great market and meeting place of Athens. It's less than half a mile from the base of the Acropolis, on one of the main streets. You wander past the farmers' markets, where you see olives, herbs, figs, grains and grapes, textiles, goats, and even slaves for sale. You pass stalls heaped with cotton and wool, woven cloth, wool blankets, and pottery. Tables and benches have been set out in the center square. You ask a man where you can get some water to drink. He points to a huge cask mounted on a large block of wood.

"Fill your flask from that," he says.

You buy some sweetened bread from a woman vendor, then fill your flask, sit on a bench, and drink the refreshing cold water.

"You must be a stranger here," your neighbor says. "My name is Nimides."

You shake the Athenian's hand. "Yes, I have come a long way. This water tastes good."

Nimides smiles. "There is no water in the world like the water of Greece, and none in Greece so fine as that in Athens."

You can't help but like this friendly fellow.

"How is it—living in Athens these days?" you ask.

"We have been through many years of war," says Nimides, "but now if the gods are willing, we shall have peace for our lifetimes. Tell me, what brings you to our city?"

"I seek to learn the secret of the Oracle," you say.

"The Oracle of Delphi?"

You nod.

"Well then," says Nimides—his eyes narrowing—"you must prepare yourself, or you will not even be allowed near the Oracle. Either you must accomplish some great feat, or you must make a large offering of gold or jewels, or you must impress the priests with your knowledge."

You lean forward and rest your hand on his arm.

"I have no gold or jewels. What shall I do?"

Nimides rubs his chin a moment. "The Pythian games will be held in a few days—they are second in importance to the Olympic games, and they are held in Delphi itself. If you could win an event in the games, I am sure the priests would let you consult the Oracle."

"Ah, I see. You also said they would be impressed by knowledge—what sort of knowledge?"

"Knowledge of Greece, of course," Nimides replies. "And for that you can do no better than to consult Thucydides. He is an old man and has many enemies, but no one knows more than he. He has written a history of the great war that wracked our land for so many years. If he's willing to talk to you, he can tell you what you need to know."

Since you have been transformed into an almost perfect human, you might be able to win at the Pythian games. On the other hand, the knowledge of Thucydides would no doubt be valuable. He is one of the men mentioned by the woman you met on the road.

If you decide to compete in the Pythian games, turn to page 27.

If you decide to seek out Thucydides, turn to page 29.

At last you reach the summit of the Acropolis. You gaze with wonder at the enormous ivory statue of the goddess Athena. Her helmet, spear, and sandals are made of solid gold. Then you turn your eyes to the great temple—the Parthenon. Statues of the gods adorn its pediment. They look like large dolls with their pink faces, their red hair, and their green and scarlet clothes; yet their shields and sandals are plated with polished gold.

Below the pediment is a beautiful band painted in bright colors against a pale blue background. You learned on Turoc that the ancient Greeks were fun-loving people and that they were also perfectionists. They wanted perfect bodies and perfect art. Certainly the Parthenon is a perfect building, you think.

A man wearing an embroidered chiton strides past. You follow him into the building. The space is crowded with people, and you have to scramble up on a wooden scaffold to see over the heads of those in front of you. A fire is roaring in an open area at the far end of the temple. You watch with amazement as a priest stands before an altar. Blood splatters his long white robe as he slits the throat of a wild boar!

Seeing another priest walking toward the entrance, you jump down from your perch and work your way toward him. He is carrying a large bowl decorated with scenes of horses and chariots.

You fall into step with him. "Sir, could you tell me how I can find the Oracle of Delphi?"

The priest stops short. "Few people are admitted before the Oracle," he says curtly. Then he eyes you curiously. "I would have taken you for a merchant from the market, or perhaps a teacher, but something tells me you are not an ordinary citizen."

If he only *knew*, you think. You wish you could tell him you're an Earth Inspector, but of course that's against the rules.

"Yes," you answer modestly, "I have come a great distance. I seek to learn the secret of the Oracle."

The priest seems startled by your words. The liquid in his bowl seethes and swirls as if beset by a miniature storm. He looks at you with awe and fear. "You were sent by Athena—for whom I have offered up this blood!" The priest raises the bowl up to the level of his eyes. "Or are you Athena transformed?"

While you are trying to think of an answer, his face turns dark. "Or—perhaps you are a runaway slave!"

"I am *not* a runaway," you say. "And who are you?"

"My name is Athos," he replies, "a priest devoted to Athena. You may stay in our quarters tonight. Tomorrow I shall join the pilgrims marching to Eleusis. It's on the way to Delphi, as you must know. Perhaps I shall accompany you to see the Oracle. I would attend your hearing with interest. If you were truly sent by Athena, you shall receive the answer you seek. If not, you shall be hurled to your death, as befits one who would profane this temple!"

You are confused by Athos and a little worried what he might do. On the other hand, he has offered to take you directly to the Oracle.

If you accept Athos's offer, turn to page 34.

If you decline, turn to page 37.

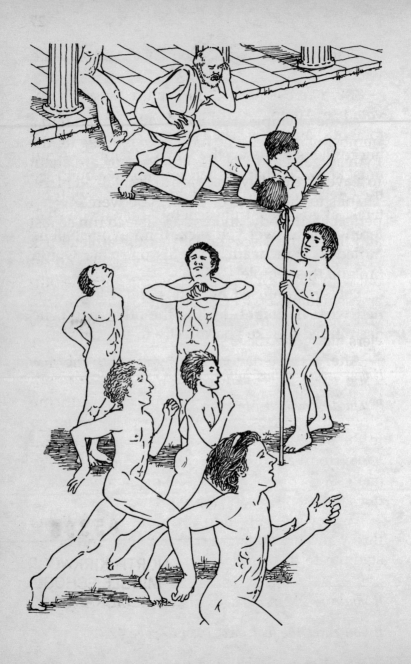

At the Olympic stadium in Athens, you find a number of athletes who have been training for the Pythian games at Delphi. In fact, they are about to leave on the sixty-mile trek to that fabled place. Thanks to the power of Turoc, you were given a perfect Earth body, and you are able to run so fast and throw the discus so far that the athletes ask you to join their group. A few days later you set out with them for Delphi. Traveling with the others, sometimes on foot, sometimes riding on carts, you are safe from the bandits who threaten travelers along the road.

After a three-day journey, you reach the majestic slopes of the sacred mountain—the hallowed shrine at Delphi. You encamp with the others in your group, and the next morning go to the stadium where officials are watching athletes from all over Greece practicing for the games. As you watch these young men, you wonder whether you can possibly win.

Two events appeal to you—one is the discus throw and the other is a race from one end of the stadium to the other.

If you compete in the discus throw, turn to page 39.

If you enter the foot race, turn to page 42.

After wandering around Athens half the day, questioning everyone who might know, you at last find the house of Thucydides. A servant greets you at the door.

"I don't think the master will see you," he says. "It's not even worth asking. Thucydides is old, and not well. He turns away most visitors."

"Please, I am a stranger from a foreign land, but I first need some special knowledge," you say. "I seek to learn the secret of the Oracle."

Giving you a skeptical look, the servant says, "Very well, wait here."

A few minutes later he returns. "When I described you to him, the master said you might be a historian, like himself. He has asked me to show you into the garden, where he will receive you."

The servant leads you into a courtyard behind the house. Amidst a cluster of potted plants and flowering trees sits a thin, gray-haired man. He seems in ill health and does not rise to greet you.

"What is it you seek of me?" Thucydides's eyes seem half closed as he speaks in a soft, hoarse voice.

"Sir, I wish to learn the secret of the Oracle: How can she foretell the future?"

Thucydides opens his eyes. "Listen to what I tell you," he says. "Have you heard of Pericles?"

You shake your head.

"Pericles was the greatest leader of Greece. He helped make Athens the most cultured and democratic city in the world."

"He must have been very wise," you say.

The old man scowls. "Yes, except for one thing: He thought that because he governed Athens so well he had the right to govern all the cities of Greece."

"Did the leaders of the other cities agree with him?"

Thucydides shakes his head. "Of course not." The old man gets to his feet, picks up a jug, and pours water onto some plants growing in clay pots nearby, then slumps into his chair with a sigh. "So Pericles failed to do what he could have done to prevent war."

"What made him think Athens would win the war?"

Thucydides shakes his head. His eyes seem filled with sadness. "Pericles had a whole list of reasons. He thought our people would be safe behind the city walls, and we could use our many ships to capture our enemies' ports."

"Did his strategy work?"

"Here's how it worked: The enemy invaded our country and cut down our orchards and burned our fields!"

"Then what happened?"

"Something unexpected, as is so often the case in war. *No matter how smart a country's leaders are, they never foresee the surprises that lie in store for them!*"

"What happened?" you ask eagerly.

The old man's fingers quiver as he speaks. "*Plague* —the most terrible pestilence you can imagine. Everywhere people lay sick and feverish, coughing, shaking, their bodies covered with sores— and the sickest of them suffering from a terrible thirst that would not go away no matter how much they drank. A third of our people died, among them Pericles himself."

"That must have been a terrible time to live through," you say. "Did the war end then?"

Thucydides shakes his head. "Except for a few short years of peace, it lasted twenty-five years more."

"It's too bad," you say, "that Pericles did not consult the Oracle of Delphi before leading Athens into war."

The historian leans toward you. His eyes are glittering as he says, "Only a few days ago, I learned from a priest who was there that Pericles *did* consult the Oracle."

"He asked the Oracle what would happen if he made war?"

Thucydides nods. "And the Oracle said, 'There

will be a great victory.' Pericles, proud man that he was, assumed that the great victory would be his!"

"That was arrogant of him," you say.

"Yes—arrogance is the greatest curse of man."

Thucydides begins to say something else, but his voice falters and his servant motions to you that it is time to leave. You go to the chair where the old man has slumped and seems half asleep.

You thank him, though you cannot be sure he hears you. Returning to the dusty streets of Athens, you think about what the Oracle said to Pericles—it might be a clue to her secret.

Turn to page 45.

The next morning Athos leads you to a place at one corner of the Agora, and you assemble with a group of pilgrims who are making the journey to Eleusis. Soon the march begins. Mingling with the crowd, you walk along the Panathenaic Way, the main road to the northwest gate of Athens, then pass through the city wall and set out across the plain towards Eleusis. It is a fourteen-mile journey, with few stops, but the other pilgrims have brought olives, grapes, and bread, and they share them freely with you. The Greeks are used to walking, and even running great distances, and they set a fast pace, stopping only every few hours at a spring to drink.

You reach Eleusis in midafternoon, entering the city through a gate in the massive stone wall around it. You follow the other pilgrims into a great building. Its enormous roof is held up by more pillars than you can count—one of the pilgrims tells you that it has the largest roof in Greece. You watch priests move from one to another of the shrines dedicated to various gods. Many pilgrims are holding torches and chanting in front of the shrine of Demeter, the earth-mother.

"Why are they doing this?" you whisper to the man standing next to you.

He looks startled for a moment, then replies, "See that shaft of wheat the goddess is holding in her hand? It is through the grace of Demeter that crops grow in the fields. Through these ceremonies, we seek her help in renewing the fertility of the earth."

"And who is that god?" you ask, pointing at a statue of a man who looks rather slight for an Olympian.

The pilgrim eyes you curiously. "Why, that is Hermes, of course, the god of heralds and merchants—everyone knows that!"

"Yes, everyone who is a Greek!" It is Athos's angry voice behind you. You turn to look at him—his eyes are blazing. "You are not even a Greek, much less a god!" he roars. He calls to a guard standing nearby. "Seize this intruder—guilty of blasphemy!"

You take no time to argue but race for the gate, dodging around dozens of startled pilgrims.

"Stop the intruder!" Athos shouts.

Fortunately, you are hidden by the crowd. Once out of the building, you run like a deer, passing through the town gates before the guards give chase.

Turn to page 47.

After leaving Athos, you're about to look into one of the other buildings on the Acropolis when you spot an old priest sunning himself in a corner of the courtyard. Thinking that he must have learned a great deal in his long years, you walk over to greet him.

"Could you give some advice to a stranger?" you ask politely.

The priest looks up.

"I want to find the Oracle of Delphi," you say, "and ask a very important question."

"Before the Oracle will answer your questions," the priest says, "you must learn how to ask the right questions. You should speak to Socrates, the philosopher. You'll probably find him in the public square framed with cyprus trees—not far from the foot of the Acropolis."

The old man's chin falls against his chest. Either he has dozed off or he simply doesn't want to talk.

Why should you have to learn how to ask questions, you wonder. It sounds like a waste of time. On the other hand, you wouldn't want to travel to Delphi and not be allowed to see the

38

Oracle. And wasn't Socrates one of those mentioned by the woman you met outside the gates of Athens?

Turn to page 52.

The next morning dawns clear and cool. The stadium is filled with spectators as you take your place in line with the discus throwers. Most of them are taller and look stronger than you.

The man ahead of you, Santos, is the champion. You watch with awe as he picks up the bronze disk, gripping it with the edges of his fingers and forearm. Slowly he turns in a tight circle, gathering speed. His arm becomes a catapult as he lets the discus fly. You watch it soar across the field as if it were free of gravity. It lands over a hundred feet away! Officials run to mark the spot where it hit.

Now it's your turn. You have a strong body and a strong arm. If you had trained for this event, you might have been the best in Greece. But throwing the discus requires not only speed but also perfect timing. You must twist in just the right way— so that all your strength is transferred into speed as your fingers release the discus.

You stand for a moment, then spin in a tight circle, gathering speed, and let the discus fly! Even as it leaves your hand, you know it will not carry more than half the distance Santos achieved.

The crowd groans as your discus hits the dirt. You walk off the field, keeping your eyes straight ahead. Later that day you try to see the Oracle, but the priest at the gate to the Oracle's chamber turns you away. "You have not yet learned the things you need to know before the Oracle will see you," he says.

Having no other choice, you set out the next morning on the long road back to Athens.

Turn to page 56.

You stand near the end of the stadium and watch the parade. The athletes march on foot. The patricians follow in their chariots. Then come trumpeters, then musicians with flutes and lyres. The sound is so lively it makes you want to dance! Though Earth people are primitive, they can make wonderful music, you think.

You've been enjoying the parade so much, you've almost forgotten that the foot races are about to begin! Your race is for the full length of the stadium—about 200 meters. You run to the starting line and slip in among the contestants. Before you even brace yourself for the start, a horn sounds and the runners are off!

You are the last to start. Running hard as you can, you slowly gain on the Greek athletes. The cheers of the crowd ring in your ears. Halfway down the track you're almost even with the leaders. You strain to the utmost, racing neck and neck against the swiftest of the Greeks, then put on a final burst of speed and cross the line! *First!* You've won!

The judges flock about you. But their faces look stern. Something is wrong. One of them tells you

that you've been disqualified because you failed to take the oath required of all contestants. You explain that you didn't hear anything about an oath. They just shake their heads. Unfair as it seems, they refuse to change the rules.

The head judge is sympathetic. He promises that you'll be allowed to compete in the next Olympics, where you will have a chance to beat the champion runner of Greece. This is nice to hear, but unfortunately, it won't do you any good now.

"Do you think I could see the Oracle?" you ask him.

"It wouldn't be wise to try on the very day you've been disqualified," he says. "Go back to Athens and return here another time."

You hear that that evening warriors will race each other while fully clothed in armor. Then, a hundred bulls will be slaughtered and their legs carried to the top of the altar and burned in honor of Apollo. You'd like to stick around for the fun, but you decide that you should not delay in setting out for Athens.

Turn to page 56.

After leaving Thucydides's house, you decide to go to the harbor at Piraeus and try to find a captain who will give you passage to Delphi.

Wending your way through the maze of streets and paths, you soon become lost. You're about to ask directions when you feel a heavy hand on your shoulder.

A burly man wearing an eye patch wheels you around. An even larger one jumps from behind a wagon.

"Get your hands off me!" you cry. "I am a visitor in this land!"

"You *were* a visitor," the man with the eye patch says. "Now you are a slave!"

They force you onto a wagon and tie you to a post so you can't escape. The wagon lumbers along a bumpy unpaved street.

"We'll be there just in time," one man says.

"Be where?"

"You'll see."

The men whip the oxen to speed them on. The cart rattles along at such speed you're afraid that a wheel will fall off. At last it pulls to a stop in front of a large oblong building made of wood and stone.

Your captors lead you inside, and you see at once that an auction is in progress—an auction of people! You have been brought to a slave mart and will soon be the property of the highest bidder!

Several men walk past, stopping to inspect you and other slaves. One of them—Demetris you hear him called—peels back your lips and looks at your teeth.

"Perfect," he says.

The bidding begins. Several men bid on you. Your price goes up and up!

Turn to page 68.

As you continue on your way to Delphi, the sea is close by on your left, but after a few miles the road turns inland and you begin to climb into the hills to the northwest—toward the city of Thebes. The road becomes pebbly and uneven. You have to be careful not to twist your ankle on a path more favorable to goats and oxen than to hikers. Fortunately, summer rains have turned the fields green. You're able to gather olives from the trees and earn meals by tending goats and helping with chores along the way, sleeping at night on mats of straw, in barns, or out under the stars.

On and on the path twists through dense forests, over shaky wooden bridges, and up and down rocky hills where wildly shaped pines shoot up out of every niche. After passing a broad, shallow lake surrounded by forest, the path turns upward. Now mountains loom on all sides. The trail dodges in and out of various ridges and spurs, and takes you high above a spectacular gorge, until finally, as you round the last towering spur of a snow-capped peak, Delphi comes suddenly into view.

You gasp at the majesty of the scene before

you, but at the same moment you hear shouting! A band of grizzled men, armed with spears and clubs, rushes you from behind. Before you can make a move, one of them has pulled you to the ground. They rip off your pack and yank out its contents.

"Where is your gold?" one shouts.

"Are you hiding your jewels?" another demands.

"No, I have nothing but a few copper coins, a water jug, and some extra clothing," you protest. "What makes you think I have gold?"

"You were going to Delphi—to consult the Oracle, right?" one man says. "You know you'll have to make an offering!"

"I thought that I might persuade them—I can give them knowledge."

"Ha!" the leader jeers at you. "What knowledge?"

"Why, knowledge about the stars," you say without thinking about it.

"How can you know any more about the stars than anyone else?" another man demands.

You wish you could tell them *why* you know so much about the stars—having recently traveled past several hundred of them.

One of the brigands cuffs you across the ear. "What a useless dolt we have here," he says.

"Worthless to us," another says.

"Let's not waste more time here."

"Just a moment," the leader says in a forceful voice. "This strange person may have no gold or jewels and yet be worth something!"

The others look questioningly at their chief.

"As a slave," he says. "Why should we have to cook our food and build huts in the woods and steal olives from the groves when we could have a slave?"

The others cheer.

The leader holds a knife to your chest. "From now on you shall be our slave. If you try to escape—you die."

He jabs the knife at you, cutting your chiton with its tip. You feel the sharp point against your skin.

Turn to page 57.

Quite by luck you happen upon a public square framed by giant cyprus trees. In one corner, a bearded man with knotted hair is surrounded by a crowd. Some people seem to be just watching, but others are talking and gesturing. You hurry toward them.

"Is that Socrates?" you ask a woman crossing the square.

"Indeed it is," she replies. "But don't think of debating him—he'll make a fool of you."

You thank her and continue toward the group, working your way through the crowd until you're close enough to hear the conversation.

A young man with flashing dark eyes is arguing with the famous philosopher. You press closer, trying to hear. They are talking about what beauty is. The young man says that either something *is* beautiful or it is not. "All you have to do is look at it to tell," he says. But Socrates confuses him with so many questions that after a while the young man admits that he can't tell what is beautiful and what is ugly!

After hearing this, you feel wary about questioning the great philosopher, but then you

remember that you have the wisdom of Turoc, and you boldly step forward.

"Sir, I am a stranger here and seek to question the Oracle of Delphi. I was told you might be able to help me know what I must say."

"And what do you plan to ask?" Socrates demands.

"I want to know the Oracle's secret—how she can foretell the future."

Socrates looks about the crowd, a grin on his face as if what you said is amusing.

"What makes you think the Oracle can foretell the future?"

"Why, because I've heard that she says things about the future and has never once been wrong."

"Suppose," says the philosopher, "I tell you that next year the sun will shine and that also it will rain. Would I be right?"

"Yes—"

"Would you say then that I can foretell the future?"

"Not just because you can tell me it's going to rain and shine next year!"

"Well then, what makes you think the Oracle can foretell the future?"

Before you have a chance to reply, others jostle in front of you, several of them talking at once. You realize you won't have another chance to question the philosopher.

A kindly looking man rests a hand on your shoulder. "That's the way it goes when one talks to Socrates," he says. "But why look so sad?"

"I've lost my chance to learn anything from him," you reply.

"Not so at all," the man says. "You've learned that asking questions can be a good way to think about things."

While you are pondering this, he adds, "If you still want to see the Oracle, you would do well to go to the docks and work your way to Delphi by boat. But if you have not yet been to the Agora, be sure to stop there first."

If you have not yet been to the Agora, turn to page 17.

If you have already been there, turn to page 93.

You're in a bad mood by the time you reach Athens. You hate starting over again. What's more, you've caught a cold—something that could never happen on Turoc! Why should being an Earth Inspector be so hard? It sounded like fun visiting Earth. You never dreamed you'd have so much trouble getting to see the Oracle. Maybe you should go back to Turoc and ask for help from the Surveyor of the Spheres.

If you have not been to the Parthenon and wish to go there and seek advice, turn to page 21.

If you return to the Voyager and embark for Turoc, turn to page 60.

The bandits take you across the ridge and lead you along an animal trail that runs through rough, scruffy woodland. The trail climbs up toward a natural limestone wall. You can't tell how high it rises, but it must be two or three hundred feet at least—impossible to climb. Where can these madmen be heading? Then you see a little stream, trickling along the base of the cliff, and the remains of a campfire. On the other side of the stream is a shallow cave, hollowed out of the limestone. Straw has been placed in different areas for beds. There are piles of clothes and food, wooden buckets, spears, knives, ropes, and other supplies. In the rear of the cave is a wooden box, closed and sealed with wax. You wonder if there might be treasure inside.

One of the bandits hovers close to you. "That's your new home," he says, motioning toward the cave. He crosses the stream, jumping from rock to rock. You and the others follow his lead.

The bandits take off their goatskin boots and relax about the cave. One of them begins striking flint to start a fire. Others unpack food they have stolen from travelers on the road to Delphi. You

are tired and would like to rest, but the leader motions you to come closer.

"Gather wood for the fire, slave," he says.

One of the others shakes a club at you—a warning of what will happen if you refuse to obey.

You start into the woods, looking for sticks and logs for the fire. No one is watching—here's your chance to escape. But you stop to think. You're in a wilderness, stripped of all supplies. You're not even sure you can find your way back to the road. If you get lost, no search party will come after you. The bandits must be sure that you can't find your way through the maze of trails, or they wouldn't let you loose.

If you try to escape, turn to page 63.

If you bide your time, turn to page 64.

As you trudge along the road out of Athens, you wave and say hello to farmers bringing their produce to market. The sun climbs higher in the sky. It gets so warm that you work up a sweat— as Earth people do—just from climbing the hill.

The slate-gray boulder is still in place. You look around to make sure no one is watching, then call on the power of Turoc. Your brain emits the coded signals that effect molecular change. In the space of a second the atoms in the boulder are recombined to form the same spacecraft that brought you to this planet. (This sort of thing is common enough on Turoc, but Earth people probably won't learn how to do it for a million years or so.) Once aboard the *Voyager*, you activate your computer with the simple command: *"Transit."*

Silently the craft lifts off, ascending so fast as to be quickly invisible to anyone standing on the ground, and you enter the space-time continuum. Later, or earlier (it doesn't matter which, when you are traveling out of time), your craft enters the silvery blue atmosphere of Turoc, the planet of shimmering sounds and muted lights—a world as different from Earth as day is from night.

Gliding through the ether, you land the *Voyager* on the grassy plain. As soon as you've transformed yourself into your own body, you glide into the Chamber of Wisdom, where the Surveyor of the Spheres awaits you.

"Well, my friend." Simbar's sonorous voice fills the room. "You have completed your mission so soon?"

"I'm afraid not," you reply. "It's very hard even to reach the Oracle, much less find her secret."

Simbar nods sympathetically. "Do not be discouraged. Earth is a strange planet—some think it the strangest in the galaxy. Tell me what happened."

As you recount your adventures, Simbar smiles knowingly. "Return to Earth," he says, "but this time do not spend your time competing in games. Instead, seek out knowledge. The Greeks value sports, but above all they value truth."

Simbar leaves the chamber even before you can thank him. His advice does not seem that helpful, but you are determined to succeed, so you board your spacecraft at once and set out again for Earth.

Sometime later (or in another instant, depending on whether you think like a Turonian or an Earthling), you land in Greece and once

62

again transform your spacecraft into a slate-gray boulder.

Again you set out for Athens. As you walk along the dusty road, you think of the woman you first met at the city gates, and of what she advised you.

Turn to page 65.

The moment you're out of sight you start running along the trail in the direction of the road. You find one fork after another in the trail. The more you look at each fork, the more confused you become.

It's getting dark. You kick at a tree stump in frustration. Seeing no other choice, you turn back to the bandits' camp. By the time you get there, the only light is from the pale half moon flickering through the trees.

The bandits are furious at you for not gathering wood.

"We have decided to go back to Athens tomorrow," the leader says. "As for you, we all agree you are useless. We're going to sell you as a slave to work in the salt mines. Some day you'll wish you were back with us!"

Turn to page 66.

Except for the flickering light of the pale half moon, it's dark by the time you're finished gathering wood. But your work isn't done. The bandits make you cook and wait on them, and give you only scraps for your dinner.

As the evening wears on, they grow jolly. "You are such a good slave," the leader says, "we could probably sell you to the richest man of Athens!"

Turn to page 66.

If you have not seen a play by Sophocles and decide to do so now, turn to page 77.

If you have not talked to Socrates and decide to do so now, turn to page 52.

If you have not talked to Thucydides and decide to do so now, turn to page 29.

If you have already done all of these things, turn to page 74.

You are forced to go with the bandits as they work their way toward Athens, traveling through the forest and robbing travelers along the road. Almost a week passes before you arrive. The bandits waste no time putting you on display at the slave market—to be auctioned to the highest bidder.

One of your captors taunts you. "Empiraeus is here," he says, "owner of the silver mines of Laurenuin. You look strong enough and he will surely buy you to work in the mines. It is a pity—you will never see the light of day again."

You shudder on hearing this, for you doubt that even the power of Turoc can save you from imprisonment deep within the earth.

A few minutes later Empiraeus looks you over, smiling as he pulls back your lips to look at your teeth.

Then the bidding begins.

"I'll bid a hundred," Empiraeus says.

A bald man with a luxuriant beard has just entered the building.

"I'll bid a hundred and twenty-five," he calls without even sitting down.

You have a glimmer of hope, for the newcomer looks much more kindly than the mine owner.

"A hundred and thirty," says Empiraeus.

"Well, Demetris?" the auctioneer says. But the bald man averts his eyes.

"Well, then—going to Empiraeus, once—twice—" The auctioneer holds his gavel over the table.

"A hundred and forty," Demetris says.

Go on to the next page.

Blonk. The auctioneer brings his gavel down. "Sold to Demetris, a patrician of Athens."

Your new owner leads you through the winding streets of Athens. Though you pass imposing temples and landscaped open spaces, most of the streets are narrow, and the houses have only plain mud-brick walls. Many of them are no more than hovels; they look as if they contain no more than a couple of dark rooms. Demetris tells you that most people spend little time in their homes except for sleeping. "The climate here is the best in the world," he says. "So most work and play takes place outside."

Entering a much richer neighborhood, you arrive at Demetris's house. It is built around a courtyard, which you reach from the street by a narrow corridor. The yard is filled with flowers and potted palms. The house itself, unlike most, is a full two stories high.

Demetris assigns you the job of preparing and serving meals and cleaning the house. You soon find you must work every waking hour, and your bed is only a pallet in a tiny room off the kitchen.

The customs of people here seem strange

compared with those on Turoc. The men and women do not spend much time with each other. The men stay in the rooms around the front courtyard. The women of the house and the young children are usually in the rear courtyard, where the cooking and weaving is done. The women sleep upstairs, which is reached by a steep, narrow staircase, while the men sleep downstairs.

The men's dining room is the largest and most impressive room in the house. Demetris's friends visit there almost every evening. They sit around for hours talking about philosophy and politics. The rooms are lit by oil lamps and torches. You have to bring food in from the kitchen and put it on small tables which you then place before the guests. Some evenings a player makes music on a lyre. Often, toward the end of the meal, a dancer and a flute player come in and entertain the guests.

The food is usually simple, mostly bread and cheese and a porridge made from barley. Once in a while Demetris throws a banquet that includes roast lamb seasoned with herbs, figs, apples, pears, and pomegranates, eggs, fish fried in olive oil, and cakes sweetened with honey. It's amazing his friends don't all get fat as a house.

The guests drink much wine, and the parties sometimes go on half the night. Demetris makes you stay up late to clean up and convert the eating couches into beds for extra guests.

It's better than working in the salt mines, but it's not fun, and you're not accomplishing your mission. Each day, as you work in the service of Demetris, you try to think of how to escape.

One morning a chance comes. Demetris has left on a journey to inspect his estates in Megarra, west of Athens. Knowing you will not be missed for a day or two, you slip out of the house.

Turn to page 65.

You're determined to get to Delphi as quickly as possible, and that means traveling by sea. You've noticed that fish are brought in to the city in carts drawn by oxen or donkeys from the port of Piraeus, five miles south of the city. The fish arrive covered with layers of burlap to keep them as cool and wet as possible. Once the fish are unloaded, the carts are returned to Piraeus, usually empty except for the cloths that were used to cover the fish. Instead of buying fish, you mingle among the crowd, pretending to be occupied with business for your master. Meanwhile, you keep an eye on the fish market. When no one is looking, you climb onto a cart and hide under the burlap cloths.

It feels cold and clammy, and the smell is terrible—worse than anything you ever experienced on Turoc. But soon the cart begins to move, rattling along the cobbled road. After a while it stops. You hear voices. You must be at the city gates. Will they be looking for an escaped slave? You don't dare breathe!

The cart is moving forward again. That means you've passed the gates! You try in vain to sleep

while the cart rattles on along the bumpy road. It seems like forever, but it's probably only an hour or so later when it stops again—this time at the gates of Piraeus! As soon as you're through them, you hop off the cart and make for the harbor, where you bathe and wash out your clothes. You pull a spare chiton and pants from your pack and change into them. At last you have a moment to look around you.

Turn to page 79.

That evening you go to the theater where the plays of Sophocles are being presented. Luckily, you arrive just as one is about to begin.

"What is the name of the play?" you whisper to the woman next to you.

"*Antigone*," she whispers back.

Fascinated, you watch the scene that unfolds before you: A great king, named Creon, has just won an important battle. One of his enemies, Polynices, lies dead upon the fields. Creon is so angry that he forbids anyone to bury the slain warrior. Antigone, Polynices' sister, naturally wants to bury him. But Creon warns her that she will be put to death if she disobeys his order. She buries him anyway.

Creon's son, Haemon, pleads with his father to spare Antigone.

"Never!" says Creon. "She has disobeyed the king. She does not deserve to live!"

A wise man comes onstage. He warns Creon that he has gone too far.

Still Creon won't give in. He locks Antigone in a cave without enough food or water for her to survive.

Not long afterward, news reaches the king that

Antigone and Haemon have slain themselves in grief. Eurydice, the king's wife, is so stricken with grief that she too commits suicide. Now Creon has lost both his son and his wife. Too late, he has learned the penalty of his cruelty and arrogance.

"I know not where to turn for help," he says. "My head is bowed with fate too heavy for me."

And so the play ends.

As you start up the steps from your seat, you overhear two men speaking.

"Creon should have consulted the Oracle of Delphi before doing what he did," one says.

"Someone asked Sophocles that very question," the other man replies. "Sophocles said that Creon *did* consult the Oracle, and the Oracle told him what would happen."

You cannot help but interrupt. "What did the Oracle predict?" you ask.

The man turns, startled a bit by your question, but then he smiles and says, "The Oracle said that the laws would be carried out."

That night you lie in a field under the stars, thinking about the Oracle's prediction. You awake in the morning refreshed and eager to finish your mission.

If you have not been to the Parthenon, turn to page 15.

Otherwise, turn to page 93.

Dozens of colorful boats are tied up at the docks. Most of them are fishing vessels. But there are several larger traders and galleys designed to be propelled by oarsmen as well as by sail. The water is as blue as the sky itself—almost motionless except for little ripples on the surface.

A man has just unloaded several barrels of fish on the dock nearest you. He's obviously pleased with his catch.

"Pardon me," you say. "I'm looking for a way to get to Delphi."

The fisherman looks you up and down. "Well, my friend, Delphi is halfway up the side of a mountain, but you can travel most of the way by sea—first on a boat to Kiras; then, after you cross the Isthmus of Corinth, on another boat to the port nearest Delphi. He points to a vessel being loaded with crates. "If you can convince the captain of that one that you are willing to work hard, I'm sure he will give you passage."

You thank the fisherman and, following his advice, earn passage on a boat bound for Kiras with a cargo of pottery. It is just a day's voyage, and a pleasant one, for the winds are fair and you pass many beautiful islands on the way. Once you're

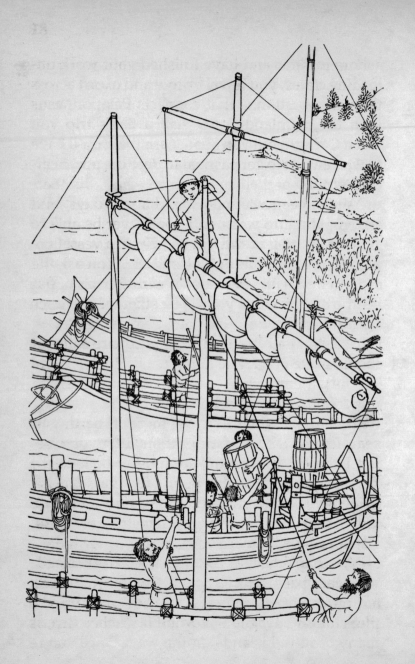

ashore in Kiras and have finished your work un-
loading crates, you travel by foot and oxcart across
the narrow isthmus that connects Peloponnesus
with the mainland. After half a day's trip you
reach Corinth, but you soon learn that you'll have
to wait awhile to get passage to Itea, the port nearest Delphi.

You've been waiting around a few days, and
are beginning to wonder if you'll ever be able to
get passage to Itea, when you hear of a vessel going there with a cargo of glazed tile. You ask the
captain if he will take you on with the crew, but
he gruffly turns you away. You stand on the dock
and look longingly at the ship, named the *Meteor*.
It has two stout masts and large square sails—it
should make good time in fair wind. You've heard
it's only a one-day passage to Itea. Maybe you
could stow away on the *Meteor*.

Deciding it's the best way to get aboard, you
start helping load on cargo. It's not easy work because the heavy crates of tile have to be lowered
deep into the hold so as to provide good ballast;
then they must be braced so that they won't crash
all over the place if the ship runs into heavy seas.
There is only one place you could possibly hide—
up in the bow where the anchor chain is stored.
No one is likely to look in the chain locker. There's
not much chance the ship will anchor during a
single day's voyage, and when it reaches Itea, it

will tie up to the dock. You won't be comfortable, hiding in the chain locker, bouncing up and down as the ship plows through the waves, but it's only for a day, and you can bring along some fruit and bread to eat. Maybe you should try it.

If you stow away on the Meteor, turn to page 94.

If you decide not to risk it, turn to page 98.

You and Xenos leave Itea at dawn. After traveling along winding, dusty roads almost all day, you stand at the foot of a great hill that rises to the north. Buildings are set at each level on the hillside. Their stone columns gleam in the sun. One temple stands out among the others. Eagerly you climb toward it—up the steep, winding path.

The shadows of nightfall are climbing up the hills when at last you stand before the temple. Many others are there who have made the pilgrimage. Xenos points to a barrel-chested man with flowing black hair.

"That is Thanatroxis," he says. "He owns a dozen vineyards, I hear, and five hundred slaves; yet even *he* must wait to see the Oracle."

You elbow your way through the crowd of pilgrims and truth seekers waiting outside the courtyard. Through a narrow opening in the wall, you see the Oracle, an olive-skinned woman wearing a long white shawl. She is sitting on a tripod built over a crevice in the rocks. Three priests stand nearby. The woman shakes and quivers. She is apparently in touch with some spirit within the earth.

Suddenly a youth is at your side. "Kalas, the high priest wishes to see you," he says.

He leads you and Xenos to another chamber, where an elderly man clad in a scarlet chiton awaits you.

"I have heard of your intrepid passage," he says. "You piloted your boat through terrible waves. Three ships were lost in that storm—two of them hurled by Aeolus onto the rocks, and one claimed by Poseidon for himself."

"It was a difficult passage," Xenos says modestly. "The worst I've ever had, but the gods were with us, and here we are before you—to ask if we may consult the Oracle."

The priest nods. "It would not be possible, but the gods must have meant you to see the Oracle, or you would have perished in that storm."

You and Xenos pass through the entrance. You step forward until you are almost next to the woman in white. You are almost close enough to touch her. You feel the cool, damp breeze blowing through the crevice in the rocks. The Oracle sits in the path of the sacred wind and sings a single, trembling note. She looks at you with large almond eyes. Is she smiling? You cannot tell, so serene is her face.

Three priests are suddenly standing beside you. "Who will be first?" one whispers.

You nod at Xenos. He steps close to the Oracle.

"My wife will soon give birth to a child. Tell me—will it be a son?"

The Oracle chants some words you cannot understand. Xenos stands, wide-eyed, waiting. At last a priest interprets.

"Xenos, the Oracle says that you will be very happy with your child."

At once another priest is leading him out. Xenos turns and smiles at you, doing a little dance as he leaves the chamber. "A son, a son! I'm going to have a son!"

You are surprised he seems so sure, but you can't think of that now. It's time to ask your question!

You step closer to the Oracle—into the path of the sacred wind. Your voice trembles as you speak. *"What is your secret? How can you foretell the future?"*

The Oracle replies with a singsong chant that you cannot understand. It continues on and on until you think she will never stop. At last she falls silent and sits motionless, as if in a trance.

You look at the priests. "What does she say? What is her secret?" you ask.

They hunch over, talking in whispers. Then one lays a hand on your shoulder and says, *"You are wise enough to know."*

You start to ask for more explanation, but the priest turns away. Attendants surround you.

They hurry you out of the chamber. Xenos is waiting for you, still excited by what the Oracle said. You're excited too, because you think you've guessed the secret of the Oracle! You're so happy, in fact, that you invite Xenos to come with you and see the future of Greece.

"See the future of Greece? That could not be possible," he says looking at you curiously, "unless you were sent by the gods!"

The next day at dawn, you and Xenos set sail for Corinth. This time fair winds and sunny skies attend you. On your arrival, the two of you leave the ship and journey by land to the place in the hills where your spacecraft rests in the form of a slate-gray boulder. You call on the power of Turoc, and the *Voyager* materializes before your eyes.

Xenos slaps his hand against his forehead. He stares at you open-mouthed.

"Now I know for certain that you have been sent by the gods!"

You would take time to explain to him that you were not sent by the gods, but you know he would never understand, so you simply say, "Climb aboard, my friend."

In a few moments, your craft is traveling through time: You and Xenos are heading toward Greece as it will be 2,400 years later—in the year 2000!

As you fly over the countryside, time reels swiftly ahead. Beneath you, the seasons come and go—marked by the snows advancing from the mountains down into the valleys every fall, and by the leafing out of trees and blossoming of flowers every spring, year after year.

Cities and villages slowly grow, and are as often destroyed—by floods, earthquakes, or fires, or by war. Armies advance. Smoke rises from the battlefields. Ships clash at sea.

You touch a button on your computron and it speaks in Greek (so that Xenos can hear the history of his country). You learn the meaning of what passes beneath you: how Greece was conquered by the Romans, then by the Byzantines, then ravaged by the Normans and the Franks, then cut up in pieces and finally taken over by the Turks; and how it was not until the nineteenth century, after more than 2,000 years of subjugation, that it became the proud, free state it is today.

You must enter Earth time again, and you select the year 2000 for a closer look. Cruising in Earth time is a problem for Earth Inspectors. There's a chance of being seen by sharp-eyed pilots and even by people on the ground. When you were first training to be an Earth Inspector, Simbar told you that it's all right if some Earth people see you, because hardly anyone will believe them, but if you remain visible too long, so many people will see you that humans will learn that you really exist. Remembering this, you resolve to cruise over Greece for only a very short while.

"*Entering the year 2000,*" the computron announces.

Xenos's eyes are glued to the window as you swoop over the countryside. Much of it is poor farming land, but you can see that Greece is still made up of beautiful mountains, beautiful valleys, and beautiful seas. Scattered about this landscape are hundreds of pleasant towns and villages. Suddenly, Athens is directly beneath you. This modern city is jammed with office buildings and apartments; its streets are clogged with traffic, its air filled with smog. Within this noisy, smelly city are vestiges of another Greece, the Greece Xenos knows, of great temples, monuments, viaducts, walls, roads, and statues—some of the finest of the ancient world.

When you land the *Voyager* on a plain near Corinth—once again in the year 400 B.C.—Xenos is in a state of shock from his ride.

"It was sad to see how much my people suffered," he says, "but I'm grateful to know that Greece at last gained its freedom."

He clasps your hands. You wish him good fortune for the rest of his life; then you set out— through space and time—for Turoc.

Go on to the next page.

What a great feeling, coasting through the silvery blue atmosphere of Turoc, knowing you've completed your mission to Earth.

You've hardly landed and transformed your body into its normal state, when friends greet you, eager to hear of your travels. But you wave and smile in Earth fashion and send thought greetings in the fashion of Turoc, for you first must report to the Surveyor of the Spheres.

Simbar is waiting when you enter the Chamber of Wisdom. Majestic in his irridescent robes, his pulsing thoughts drawn into speech, he greets you.

"Welcome home, worthy friend. Let us hear your report."

"I have visited the Oracle. At first I was confused by what she said, but then I guessed her secret."

"What is it?"

"I think that the reason the Oracle can foretell the future is that the priests who interpret her are very wise, and they think up answers that can be true whatever happens."

"That's very interesting," Simbar replies, "but why does anyone believe such ambiguous answers?"

"I think it's because people hear what they want to believe. For example, Pericles asked the Oracle whether he would be victorious in war. The Oracle answered, 'There will be a great victory.' Pericles assumed wrongly that the victory would be his. Creon asked the Oracle if he could forbid the burial of the dead. The Oracle answered, 'The laws of the gods shall be upheld.' Creon assumed wrongly that the Oracle meant *his* laws, as king. Then my Greek friend, Xenos, asked the Oracle if a son would be born to his wife. The Oracle answered, 'You shall be very happy with your child.' Xenos assumed that meant his wife would give birth to a boy. Maybe she will, but from what I know of Xenos, he will be a happy father whether his next child is a boy *or* a girl."

"I see what you mean," Simbar says. "If his wife does give birth to a girl, Xenos may be disappointed for a while, but, being the good man he is, he will soon become happy with his new baby, and the Oracle will have been right after all."

"Exactly," you say.

"Well," says Simbar, "It looks as if the Oracle of Delphi does not defy the laws of science."

"Even so," you say, "I think the priests of Delphi will keep their secret for a long while, because they do not make foolish predictions but speak words of wisdom."

"I agree," says Simbar. "Earthlings should listen to such wisdom more carefully and not just hear what they want to believe." Simbar shakes your little Turonian hand. "I'm glad you had a good trip to Earth."

"Thank you, Simbar. Best of all, I liked nearly all the Earthlings I met."

He smiles at you. "Well, you'll be meeting more very soon. There's a lot more of Earth to be inspected!"

The End

You sleep that night on a straw mat in a stable. When you awake the sun is already high in the sky. A bird is singing in every tree.

Eager to be on your way, you set out at once for Piraeus, arriving there after a two-hour walk.

Turn to page 79.

Having learned that the *Meteor* is leaving at dawn the next day, you fill your pack with fruit, bread, and a cask of water. You catch a few hours of sleep in a nearby shed, then get up about midnight and return to the dock. Except for the bright stars overhead, the only light comes from a campfire near the entrance to the harbor and from the glint of phosphorus on the wavelets slapping against the dock.

Gingerly you stand on a wooden bitt around which is tied one of the *Meteor*'s mooring ropes. From there a good leap carries you up onto the ship's deck. As you land, you grab hold of the stay supporting the foremast, but the deck is slippery; your feet slide out from under you. As you fall, your knee bangs into an iron cleat. You jump up, rubbing your knee, setting a barrel rolling across the deck. Someone shouts from below.

"Who's there?"

Then—footsteps. A big man with a hairy chest towers above you. You run for the rail, but before you can jump, he shoves you hard, tumbling you over the side. You bounce off the mooring rope and onto the dock. Your head strikes the mooring bitt as you land, knocking you cold.

You awake at dawn, bruised and aching, just in time to see the *Meteor* heading out of the harbor under full sail. You struggle to your feet, but you can't walk—your ankle is badly sprained, if not broken, and your head is aching so much you couldn't walk anyway.

A man is standing next to you. A woman behind him is tending two children. The youngest is panting as if short of breath.

"My name is Kamiros," he says. "And this is my wife, Zante. My family and I are journeying to Epidaurus, the sanctuary of Asclepius, the god of healing. Our youngest child—Boetia—has trouble breathing. You too are not well, I can see. Come with us—it shall be good luck for us and for you too."

Since there is nothing else you can do, and right now you can't even think straight, you let Kamiros help you up into his cart. There you ride with the sick child while the rest of the family walks alongside as you journey along a dirt road through the forested hills that run southeastward along the seacoast. The ride is a bumpy one, but the tall, graceful trees and the cool, pine-scented air soothe you as much as any medicine. From time to time the view opens up and you can look down a thousand feet at the waves crashing against the rocky shore. On the other side of the ridge is a green valley that seems flooded with pale white light. You spot a herd of black goats far below. They look no bigger than ants—they must be miles away—yet you can hear the sound of their bells drifting up from the valley on an unseen zephyr of air.

Rounding a bend in the road, you see Epidaurus—the stadium, temples, a huge stone cistern, the baths, the landscaped sanctuary and gardens, and a huge theater set into the hillside. You count the sixty crescent-shaped rows of seats that rise steeply upward from the circular stage.

"That theater has been here for over two hundred years and there is none finer in Greece," Kamiros says. "It's too bad that the festival is not being held this month or you could see our finest games and music and plays."

"It's the most beautiful place I've seen on Earth," you say.

"That's why it's a place of healing," says Zante.

The cart descends a steep, deeply rutted road. A long, low stone building comes into view.

"This is where we may stay, along with other pilgrims," Kamiros says. "We have brought a sufficient offering so that you can stay here too."

In the morning your headache is gone, and you're able to walk with only a little pain. You stay for three more days at Epidaurus, visiting the temple of Asclepius and strengthening your ankle by walking in the forest and down to the sea. You are soon feeling better than ever, and Kamiros's child is breathing more easily too. Is this because of the healing powers of the god Asclepius, or for some other reason? you wonder. In any event, your health is restored, and Boetia has also recovered. Kamiros and his family give you a ride on their way back to Corinth. There you thank him and Zante for their kindness, and they in turn bid you good fortune in your quest.

Go on to the next page.

Two weeks pass while you wait in Corinth for a boat. In the meantime you earn a living by tending nets on a fishing boat, the *Pelican*. As so often is the case, luck comes from an unexpected source. When Xenos, the *Pelican*'s captain, learns that you wish to question the Oracle, he becomes very interested.

"What is it you wish to know?" he asks. "I have a question myself."

"I wish to learn the secret of the Oracle," you say. "And what about you?"

"More than anything else," he says, "I would like to know the future of Greece. But there is one thing I'd like to know even more than that."

"What is that, Xenos?"

"I want to know whether I shall have a son. I already have two beautiful little girls. My wife will give birth in a few months. And more than anything else I want a son."

"Then I hope your wish will be granted," you say. "Let's sail to Itea, then, and climb the hill to Delphi, and see if we can talk to the Oracle."

Xenos pounds the rail of his boat with his big leathery hand. "We'll do it!"

Setting out the next morning, you sail with

Xenos westward along the main waterway of Greece, the long, narrow gulf that separates Peloponnesus from the mainland. The weather is sparkling clear and you can see mountains on both sides of the gulf, the highest of them capped with snow. You enjoy the sail as the wind picks up and speeds the *Pelican* along. But that night you dream that the Greek gods are tossing you about. When you wake up, the boat is pitching and rolling so much it's a wonder you didn't roll out of your bunk.

Once on deck, you shiver in the damp, blustery wind blowing down from the mountains. The sea is a mass of foam and spray. Though you know the sun has risen, the sky is still dark. You cling to the mast as a wave climbs up on deck and threatens to roll the boat over. Xenos looks worried. You wonder if you'll ever see Turoc again.

The storm grows worse. One great wave after another shakes the boat. It begins to fill with water. The seamen bail frantically. Hour after hour the gale howls while they struggle to keep the vessel afloat.

"It's no use!" the mate yells over the wind.

Suddenly the lookout cries: "Cape of Nicolaos—off the starboard bow!"

A rocky spit of land looms out of the mists.

"Steer to port!" Xenos yells, "or we'll be on the rocks!"

A huge wave is bearing down.

The helmsman is losing control.

You press your own weight against the heavy wooden tiller. Short, steep waves pitch you in all directions. The boat shudders from the force of each wave, but you hold the course, though you're blinded with spray and wind-swept rain.

Then suddenly the boat steadies!

"We're past the cape!" Xenos cries. "We're in safe water." He does a little dance and hugs you. "Your presence pleased Poseidon, my friend. He tested us but did not destroy us, and Aeolus, god of the winds, drove us safely through the waves. Surely we shall see the Oracle now, and our questions will be answered!"

Though the wind still howls, the water is much calmer now that you're past the cape, and a few hours later your boat is safely docked in Itea.

"Xenos," you say, "if we had sailed more to the right we would have been dashed on the rocks, and if more to the left, we would have sunk beneath those great waves." You pat your friend on the back. "Xenos, you are a great Earth person."

"Earth person—what is that?"

"I mean a great Greek," you say.

"I thank you," he says. "Tomorrow we shall see the Oracle."

Turn to page 83.

Edward Packard is a graduate of Princeton University and Columbia Law School. In 1969, while telling bedtime stories to his children, he conceived of the idea of written stories in which the reader is the protagonist and makes choices affecting the plot, leading to multiple endings. Though his first book did not find a publisher for many years, Packard has since written over thirty others, and the interactive genre of fiction has been shown to appeal to children around the world.

Mona Conner, a freelance illustrator, graduated from The School of Visual Arts in New York City. Her illustrations can be seen on many books covers and in magazines.

Barbara Carter is a freelance illustrator living in Randolph, Vermont.

Catalog

If you are interested in a list of fine Paperback
books, covering a wide range of subjects
and interests, send your name and address,
requesting your free catalog, to:

McGraw-Hill Paperbacks
11 West 19th Street
New York, N.Y. 10011